Tom and Pippo Read a Story

PIPPO

HELEN OXENBURY

DISCOVERY TOYS

I like to look at books,
but best of all I like to
look at books with Daddy.

Daddy likes to look at his paper,
but he doesn't mind reading
my books to me.

When Daddy's finished reading
to me, I think Pippo would
like to hear a story.

So I bring Pippo
and ask Daddy to read to him.

When Daddy
says he really
can't read any
more books, I
read to Pippo.

I hope one day Pippo
can read on his own.